ONLY PIECES

edd tello

An imprint of Enslow Publishing

WEST **44** BOOKS™

**Please visit our website, www.west44books.com.
For a free color catalog of all our high-quality books,
call toll free 1-800-398-2504.**

Cataloging-in-Publication Data

Names: Tello, Edd.
Title: Only pieces / Edd Tello.
Description: New York : West 44, 2022. |
Series: West 44 YA verse
Identifiers: ISBN 9781978596016 (pbk.) | ISBN
9781978596009 (library bound) |
ISBN 9781978596023 (ebook)
Subjects: LCSH: Children's poetry, American. |
Children's poetry, English. | English poetry.
Classification: LCC PS586.3 T455 2022 | DDC
811'.60809282--dc23

First Edition

Published in 2022 by
Enslow Publishing LLC
29 East 21st Street
New York, NY 10011

Editor: Caitie McAneney
Designer: Tanya Dellaccio

Photo Credits: Cover, pp. 2-185 Olgastocker/
Shutterstock.com

Printed in the United States of America

CPSIA compliance information: Batch #CW22W44: For further information contact
Enslow Publishing LLC, New York, New York at 1-800-398-2504.

To my mamá, who truly believed in my passion for reading since I was five.

To my dad, for taking me to a bookstore so I could understand its magic for the first time.

HOME

It's Saturday.
Seven a.m.

The first rays of sun
sweep through
the broken blinds
of our crummy apartment.

The phone rings.
Amá quickly gets up.

I lie in bed.
My eyes are red.
I didn't sleep well.

I manage to
go to the kitchen.

Amá is crying.
She covers her mouth.

I think it's Grandma
she's talking with.

She cries every time
they speak on the phone.

It's been five years
since Abuela last visited us.
We were living in Texas
back then.

But this time,
Amá's face
doesn't look sad.

She hangs up.

It was your father.
He's coming home.

What?
I ask.
Just to make sure
I heard it right.

He's in Bakersfield, mijo.
We will pick him up.
Hurry.
Put some shoes on.

I puff out my chest
and put some jeans on
that my dad gave me
two birthdays ago.

I take
my writing journal
I left
on the floor last night.

Amá washes her face
and mops the floor
a little bit.
She's ready in 10.

A BETTER LIFE

We haven't seen Apá
since we moved out
last January.

We moved to Arvin
'cause my aunt Rosario
told Amá
she could find
more opportunities
in this part
of the country
                    a w a y   f r o m   A p á.

He stayed in Texas
for a construction job.

Since both
Amá and Apá
are undocumented,
EVERYTHING
is harder for them.

They need to use
other people's names
and papers to work,
or get paid cash.
Amá's English
is not very good.

She doesn't
understand English
as well
as I do.

She doesn't
go to school
as I do.

My parents
crossed the border
looking for
a better life.

*We did this
for you,*
Mom always
says.

Truth is,
life is not perfect
here.
At least
not for me.

Apá's job finished
some weeks ago.
He couldn't find
a new project,
so he's coming
home.

We will live
together
at least.

Amá's car starts
making noises.

I hope
we don't get stranded
on the road.
It happened
to us once.

It's only
30 minutes
from Arvin
though.

Amá and I
don't talk at all.

I open my notebook
and write.

"THOUSANDS OF PIECES"

a poem by Edgar Jimenez

Sunday afternoon
in the living room.
I'm five years old.

Dozens of pieces
are jumbled
on the floor.

Todas las piezas
deben encajar,
Apá starts.

I already know
all the pieces
must fit.
I do puzzles
in Kindergarten.

Sunny Sunday
on the front porch.
I'm nine.

People setting up
outside their houses
to talk and grill.

Hundreds of pieces
lined up on
the plastic table.

Apá sits
in front of me.
We begin with
the corner pieces.

One day,
I will buy you
one like this,
I say,

pointing out
a big mansion drawn
on the puzzle box.

One month ago,
I bought a puzzle
of the universe.
It still lies closed
under my bed.

Honestly,
I never was good
at puzzles.
Even when we did
the same ones
over & over again.

What I used to love
is how Apá
watched me grow
through those
thousands of pieces.

YOU WRITE
TOO MUCH

Amá says.
Tu cabeza will explode.

But when my head fills with
                     t h o u g h t s
the ideas naturally
                       f l o w.
And I can't
                       S T O P.

I roll down the window,
but I'm still sweating.

Summer hits hard.

I'm also hungry,
but I shut my mouth.
I'm just excited
to see Apá.

APÁ

Apá is already
waiting for us
on a street corner
downtown.

He's only carrying
one bag
and tiredness
over his shoulders.

His eyes have
more wrinkles
around them
than I remember.

Apá always says
they are
because of
the pounding of
a lifetime.

His brown skin
looks darker
than usual.
Probably
from spending hours
and hours
working under
the blazing sun.

Apá has
rough hands.
Amá says
they are
from working hard.

However,
his black mustache
looks untouched.

Mijo,
he wraps me
into a hug
and says
no more.

Amá hugs him
tight
and cries
on his shoulder.

We walk
a few blocks to
where we left
Amá's old
white Nissan.

Give me the keys.
I'm going to drive,
says Apá.

He thinks
the man should
always drive.

UGH,
I don't like
his macho
attitude!

*It would be best
if you rest,*
says Amá.

I'm not tired,
says Apá.

No seas terco, Pedro,
says Amá.

She's right.

Apá is very stubborn.

A SECRET

Apá turns the AC on.
It only blows out
hot air.
He looks upset.

Amá calls to me
from the passenger seat.

Edgar, your dad will stop.
The car needs gas.

I only say
OK.

We reach a gas station.

Apá stops the car
and gets out.

When I open the door,
my mom calls out
my name again.

Yes, Amá?

Don't talk
to your father yet.
He's too stressed.

She knows
my secret.

She knows
I'm dying
to say,
Apá,
I'm gay.

Ay, mijo,
you're not gay.
You're just
confused,
Amá constantly
says.

I walk toward
the store.

She winds down
her window.
Edgar?

I sigh.

Por favor,
Amá says.
Let's keep this
between us
for now,
OK?

AMÁ NEVER STOPS

Apá and I
hop in the car.

I hold some
spicy snacks
and two cokes,
one for me,
and one for Amá.

I forgot
to bring napkins,
so I lick
my greasy fingers.

Stop licking your fingers!
Don't be sucio,
Amá shouts.

Leave him alone, Lidia,
Apá responds.

He will dirty this shirt!

Amá never stops.

CLEAN

The aparment smells
like detergent
when we arrive.

Amá likes to clean.

She does babysitting
in the mornings
and sometimes
cleans houses
for some extra cash
in the afternoons.

She cleans there
and cleans here.

I'm glad
this house only has
two bedrooms,
a kitchen,
and a living room,
so she doesn't need
to clean much more.

When I offer to help,
Amá always says NO.

She has
strong arms
and legs.
Maybe that's why
she never
gets tired
or complains.

Apá places his bag
on the old couch.

Don't put it there, Pedro.
Don't you see
I just cleaned?

Apá sighs.

A FIGHT

Amá starts cooking.

Salsa verde
and onion smell
fill the kitchen.

I cough.
The chile aroma
is strong.

You need help?
I ask Amá.

Just set the table,
she says.

Amá pours the nopales
into a bowl
and chops the aguacate.

I put the corn tortillas
in the tortilla warmer.

Apá stares at the table.
No meat or chicken today?

Amá shakes her head
and says,
Only nopales, black beans,
and guacamole.
We don't have anything else.

Apá seems upset.

Amá ignores him.

There's never enough
food at home!
he exclaims.

This is not a restaurante,
plus you didn't send
the rent payment
last month,
Amá yells.

We haven't even started
eating yet, and
they're already fighting.

I eat so fast that
I almost choke.

I finish eating soon
and head to my room.

HIDDEN

I take a long nap
until the moon peeps.

My door pushes open.

Take the trash out.
It's Amá.
She never knocks.

I take the trash
to the rusty dumpster
outside
of our apartment
complex.

Suddenly,
I look at a shadow
walking d
        o
          w
            n the stairs.

It gets
closer and closer…

I get scared.

It's a boy
wearing a hoodie.
He turns left
and turns right,
like making sure
no one sees him.

Until his eyes
meet mine.
I can see them
through
the dark.

He pulls his hood off.
It's Alex Cisneros.

What is HE
doing HERE?

ALEX

I met him
on the first day
I arrived at school.

I couldn't ignore
his brown-hazel eyes and
the dimples that came out
every time he smiled.

I looked from my locker
at his ebony hair
and his light
brown skin.

But later that day,
I found out
he was friends with Tyler
and all the popular kids.

And I understood
we were pieces
from different puzzles:

Me, a kid with no friends.
Him, part of the football team.

The only thing
we had in common
was our skin color.

ANOTHER SECRET

I don't understand
why Alex is
in this part of town.

He has a lovely house
to live in and
a happy family.

Alex is wiping
his face off.
Has he been crying?

Hey man,
he says, friendly.
You're Edgar, right?

He remembers
my name.
Alex Cisneros
remembers my name!

I nod.
And you're Alex.
I speak too fast.
I notice
he wants to laugh.

You don't live here,
do you?
I ask.
He shakes his head.

Then silence.

Just visiting someone,
Alex finally says.

I want to ask
who.
But there's no need,
'cause

Alex places his hands
inside the hoodie
and says,
Actually, it's my dad.
He is living here.
My parents are…

Then more silence.

I look away.

He takes a deep breath.
Could you please
not tell anyone?

Only my best friend
knows.

I won't,
I respond.

A hundred questions
fly around my head like,
Are his parents getting divorced?
Did they fight like mine?

Guess I'll see you around,
he says.

Sure.
It's the only thing
that comes out
of my mouth.

Another secret
to keep
inside my mind.

BREAKFAST

The morning light
reflects off
Amá's long black hair
and her freshly
ironed shirt.

She's on the couch
getting ready for work.
Her licuado de papaya
sits on the scratched table
for an energy boost.

I didn't want
to wake your dad,
she speaks softly.

Don't worry.
Apá sleeps like a rock.
You should rest, too.
It's Sunday, Mom,
I whisper hoarsely.

No time for that.
We need to pay the rent,
she says
while combing her hair.

I have my part-time job.
I could help, too!
I say.
Amá hushes me.
She says I need
to save money
for my studies.

You know
how you can help?
Making breakfast
for your dad.

Do we still have eggs?
I ask.

Sí. En el refrigerador.

I open the fridge.
Only two eggs left.
I guess I will have
cereal again.

And don't eat
those Cheerios, Edgar,
Amá yells
from the bathroom.
That's not a real
breakfast.

But how can I tell her
there's nothing else?

I don't want to
put more pressure
on her shoulders,
so I turn the stove ON
before she goes.

BROKEN

When Apá wakes up,
breakfast is ready.

I managed to make
the most out of:

> two eggs,
> some refried beans,
> and the nopales leftovers.

Amá had
a piece of dough
in the fridge,
so I made gorditas.

Apá is already
at the table,
waiting.

I place the gorditas
on two plates.
He takes one,
and it breaks.
Sorry, Apá.
They're not as good as
the ones Amá makes.

He shrugs.
At least they taste fine.
He bites
the second one,
and the nopales come out
over the sides.

I let out
a nervous laugh.

Apá huffs.

Apá used to make jokes
about everything,
but he's not the same
since he came home.

We eat in silence.

Like my gorditas,
I guess he's kind of
broken, too.

LUCKY

On Monday,
I walk along
to the bus stop.

It takes me
20 minutes
to get to work.

My green shirt
is covered in sweat
when I arrive
at the store.

I look at the
big green logo.
I wish I was lucky enough
to have a dollar tree.

My friend Alison
is outside,
waiting for me.
She works next door.

She wears
her uniform.
Her hair

pulled up in a bun.
Ali irons her hair
every day,
even when
she has this job
where she's
greasy and gross
because of the endless
burgers and fries orders.

*Aren't you supposed to
be at work already?*
I ask.

She shrugs.
I'm late anyway, so…

Why are you late?
I ask, surprised
'cause she's always
on time.

*My mom
covered the night shift,
and I took care
of Leonardo.*

*He cried all night long,
asking for Mom.*

Be glad
you don't have siblings.

I giggle.
Well, I still can.
Amá is young,
and she and Apá…

Alison makes
a disgusted face.
OK, stop.

I laugh.

So, what's new?
Alison asks,
looking at her phone.

I want to tell her
about Alex visiting his dad
the other night,
but I promised him
not to tell anyone.

I say,
Apá isn't used to
living with us.
He has no job and is
always upset.

She says,
When Papá abandoned us,
it took a lot for Mom
to figure things out,
you know?

She lets out a sigh.

I mean,
nothing has changed.
Her boyfriend Gustavo
is a useless mess.

Talking with Ali
makes me realize
how lucky I am
for having
Apá and Amá.

BUS STOP

Splashes of
purple, orange, and blue
paint up the sky.

People gather
at the bus stop.

They look exhausted.
Although it was a busy day
at the store,
I'm not tired at all.

The fresh air
clears out my mind.
I start typing a poem
on my phone
on my way home.

The poem is about
Amá and Apá.
And the moon
and the sun.

Inspired by
a Mexican legend
that Abuela told me about.

"THE MOON AND THE SUN"

a poem by Edgar Jimenez

A young man
with golden hair
named Sun

and a beautiful
black-haired woman
named Moon

were deeply in love.

Universe called them
one day
when He was creating
the world.

Universe told them
they couldn't be together
anymore.
Sun will protect his kingdom

during the day.
While Moon
will be the queen of the night.

The stars as company
were not enough for her.
Moon felt alone.

But their love
shone brightly,
more intense
than anything else.

Therefore
eclipses were born...

ECLIPSE

I get off the bus
and walk home.

Amá is at the dining table
with a calculator, all stressed.
Apá is watching TV
with a beer by his side.

I walk to my room.

And I wonder
if I can be the eclipse
that keeps together
my Sun and my Moon.

I wonder
if I'm good enough.

THE PERFECT WIFE

The week disappears
beneath my feet.

On Friday night,
Amá starts
making sopes for dinner.

Oil spits everywhere
when she puts them
in the comal.

Worry brushes over
Amá's face.
She wants to be
what she thinks is
the perfect wife.

At least the sopes
look thick and round,
not like my horrifying attempt
to make gorditas.

Can I help?

Amá dries off her forehead
with her mandil.

Yes. Help me to set the table,
she says.

But I want to learn to
make sopes.
I say.

Ay, Edgar.
After the mess you made
with the gorditas?
She smiles.
I should have known better.
You're a man.
Men don't know
how to make sopes or gorditas.
But don't worry.
You will have a wife for that.

The word *wife*
is like a stab.

I exhale.
That's exactly it!
I don't want to have a—

Are you gonna
set the table or not?
Amá snaps.

What's going on?
Apá shows up.
I leave in a huff and take
the forks and knives with me.

Amá covers the sopes
with paper towels
to absorb the excess fat.

THEY DON'T UNDERSTAND

I ran into Rosario today.
She said there's a job
in the grape field,
Amá says.

Apá puts crema in his sopes.
Tell your sister
to stay out of this.

No seas grosero, Pedro, Amá says.
She only wants to help.

I'm not rude, Apá says.
It's just if she really wants to help,
she can send money
for the rent.

Amá looks at the ceiling
and sighs.

So, how's school, mijo?
Apá asks.
What do you want to study
after high school?

There's no rush.
He still has another year to go,
Amá says.
She's scared that I'll mess it all up.

Well,
I clear my throat.
I was being honest
when I said
I want to study literature.

Could you
pass me the salsa?
Apá asks Amá,
ignoring me.
I'm sure both
Amá and Apá think
I'm nuts.

I know
you like to write and read
and all those things,
but that won't give you
anything to eat, says Apá.

Amá says,
I already told him.
People don't make a living
with that unless
they're García Márquez
or Octavio Paz.

*What do you actually want
to do for a living?*
Apá asks
a second time.

They don't get it.
But how could I judge them?

Amá used to be
an elementary teacher
in Mexico.
Now she scrubs
people's floors
and cleans babies' poops.

Apá has worked
since he was
12 years old.

I know
they want the best for me.
But still,
I feel disappointed and sad.

They work so hard
for so little money.
It's not exactly
the life I want.

I take a deep…
                    …DEEP breath.

I will apply
for a scholarship.
I want to go to Oakland
or San Francisco.

Apá says,
You need to study hard,
so you can work in an office
with AC and free coffee.
Not like me, who already has
back problems.

I take the empty dishes
over to the sink.
Just like my dreams,
they land with a *crash*.

A BETTER EXCUSE

Amá and I
do the dishes.
She washes,
and I dry.

From the kitchen window,
I see a car parked.
I have seen it at school.
It's Alex's Altima.

I need an excuse
to go outside.

But there's no
trash to take out.
There are
no leftovers to toss.
If I want to go and say hello,
I need a better excuse.

Amá is washing
the last of the dishes
when I say,
I think I need some air.

Apá laughs
from the couch.
Some air?
See, Lidia?
I leave you with this kid
for some months,
and he starts acting
all agringado.

Amá carefully places
the plates on the dish rack.

It's late, Edgar, she says.
This isn't a safe place.
There are borrachos
out there.

I shake my head.
I'll be back in a minute.
I promise.

I take my poetry journal
and leave the apartment
before she says no.

AS I WAIT

I open my journal.
The streetlight is too dim.
I can't see a thing.

What if a drunk man shows up,
just like Amá said?
I should probably get back.

I close the journal,
but I keep standing on the stairway.
At least if a borracho approaches,
I'd have the chance to run.

I wait.

I pull out my phone.

                    I wait.

A little bit more.

                                        I wait.

But Alex doesn't come.
When I'm about to give up,
a light outside
Alex's dad's apartment
turns ON.
It's him.
He looks mortified.

I wish I could run,
but I feel like my feet
are glued to the floor.

It's too late.
He raises his hand
to wave.

I do the same.

ACT NORMAL

Alex walks up to me.

I barely breathe.

act normal
act normal
act normal

What up?
He smiles.

I can't take my eyes off
the tiny moles
on his neck.
They are like
a constellation
I want to trace.

Hey,
I gulp.

act normal
act normal
act normal

Visiting your dad?
I immediately
realize it was
a dumb question
to ask.

Yeah. But leaving now.
What are you up to?

I look upstairs,
making sure
Amá isn't coming.
Just writing.
I lift my journal
awkwardly.

Oh, cool.
What do you write?

My chest tightens.
He sounds waaay
more interested
than my parents.

Um, I write mostly poetry,
I say, my voice quiet.
Sometimes I write things
based on legends.

Alex grabs his chin.
Oh, I remember!
You're in the writing club!

My cheeks go hot.
Yeah.

Can I read
at least
one of your poems?
he asks,
looking at my journal.

No! I blurt out.
I mean, I have to edit them first.

He laughs.
I laugh, too.

That's OK, he says.
Take your time.
What is the one
you're writing about now?

I look back
at the stairs.
It's, um,
about my parents
and a Mexican
legend.

I shake my head.
*Promise you
it's nothing fun.*

His eyes sort of
light up.

*Well, sounds like
a big deal to me.
I would like to read it
one day.*

Nobody,
not even Alison,
has asked to read
my writing EVER.

But then
my phone buzzes
inside my shorts.
It's Amá
who's calling.

*Hey, I think I gotta go.
My mom…*

Of course.
He grins.
*Meet back here
tomorrow?*

My phone
keeps buzzing,
but I'm only focused
on what Alex just said.

act normal
act normal
act normal

Yeah. Sure,
I say.

*Are you down for
a bike ride?*
he asks.

Then I think of
my rusty old bike,
and I feel
embarrassed.

Alex looks behind me.
I turn back.
Amá is there,
with one hand
on her hip.

I can't act normal
anymore.

AMÁ IS WEARING

her cotton-knit nightgown
and her chanclas.

I wish the earth
would suck me up.

I sigh.
*Alex, this is my mother,
Lidia.*

Amá's voice is
controlled.
*Lidia Ramos,
mucho gusto.*

They each
hold out a hand.

I have to go,
Alex says,
looking at his phone.

Amá nods.
*It's late for you
to be out here.*

My dad lives here.
Alex points to his
dad's apartment.

We fall silent.

. . .

I want to walk away.

Gusto en conocerla,
Alex finally says
with this accent that
makes it obvious
he doesn't speak
Spanish at home.

Nice to meet you, too,
Amá says.

Alex unlocks his car.
See you tomorrow then.

I just nod.

Amá gazes over at me,
then starts up the stairs.

I turn back to Alex
before climbing up.

HOME IN SILENCE

The only noise
is Apá's snores
from the room.

Who was that boy?
Amá whispers.

Alex.
Just a friend
from school.

And my crush
since we moved here,
I wanna say.
I keep that part to
myself.

She huffs.
If there's something
that annoys me, it's
when you don't answer
the phone.
It really gets on
my nerves!

I roll my eyes.
Amá, please.
I always pick up.
We were just talking and—

She snaps,
If you're not going
to use it, give it to me.
I could sell that phone
in one of those
mobile stores.

I close my eyes.
Take a breath. Hold it.
Good night, Amá.
I'm done.

Come back here!
Amá is trying
so hard not to scream.
Un día me vas a matar
de un coraje!

Every time she gets upset,
she says one day
I will kill her of anger.

I think
she's just being dramatic.
I slam my door.

I HOPE

Saturday morning,
duranguense music
wakes me up.

I get scared when
Amá has the music
loud on weekends.

It scares me that
Doña Mary,
our chismosa neighbor,
calls the cops and
complains.

Doña Mary likes gossiping
about everything
that happens around her.

I constantly think
about how my parents
are here illegally and
can get deported.

I pray and hope
the migra never knocks
on our door.

GROUNDED

I walk into the kitchen.

Amá is mopping the floor.

Estás castigado,
she blurts out.

Instead of saying
good morning
      OR
              do you want some breakfast?

You're grounded
is the first phrase
she exclaims.

I already want to
go back to my room
and sleep until noon.

But then she asks me
to take a look
at the frijoles,
so they don't burn.
On weekends,
when Amá doesn't work,
she helps out the church

and makes food
for the refugee comedor
with other Catholic ladies.

Amá always asks me
to go with her.
I always think of
excuses not to go.

Sometimes
I end up giving in.
Can I ask WHY
I'm grounded?

Amá drops the mop.
Really, Edgar?
After being so rude
last night and
slamming the door,
you're asking me WHY?

I wasn't rude.
I was just…
You know, Amá?
Can't argue with you.

She folds her arms.
Fine.
Give me your phone.

No calls
        OR
                making plans.

I start to panic.
Amá, pero…

She says,
Shh. No buts!

I wish I could SHOUT,
but only a snort
comes out.

AMÁ BOILS

tomatillos and serrano peppers.

My eyes fill with tears.

Apá, freshly showered,
sits and drinks his coffee.

I pour myself
a glass of orange juice.

I'm not really hungry today,
I say.
*I don't feel like eating
enchiladas or eggs.*

Amá exhales and
shakes her head.

*You should
thank God that
we have food to eat.*

I hate when Amá
twists my words.

I'm never allowed
to say what I feel
or hide what I don't want.
I feel like one day,
like the tomatillos
or
the serrano peppers,
I will boil, too.

And I will end up saying
all those things I know
I will later regret.

When Amá goes
and checks if the veggies
are fully cooked,
I head to my room.

PRETEND

I plop down in bed.

Without a phone,
I can't text Alison
or anyone.

What worries me
the most is
I can't text Alex
and tell him
I'm grounded.

Even if
I had my phone,
I couldn't.
I forgot to ask
for his number.

This is all Amá's fault.

I don't understand
why she's so dramatic.
Are all mothers like her?

Alison goes out
and drinks
and smokes weed
and her mom never
says a word.
Maybe she doesn't know.
Maybe she PRETENDS
she doesn't know.

The same way Amá
pretends I'm not gay.

Sometimes
I wish I could run away.

VIDEO GAMES

I lock my door.

At least Amá
didn't take
the console away.

I turn it ON.

Playing video games
feels like an escape.
I imagine other worlds,
other universes.

Suddenly,
I find myself
thinking of Alex.

Fantasizing
about other school guys.

And something happens
in my body
that forces me to press
PAUSE.

I place the controller
over a poetry book
and pull my shorts off.

The church teaches us
this is gravely wrong.
But what if
it makes me feel right?

I keep going and
let my mind fly.

APÁ'S PERMISSION

Now that Amá is gone,
I leave my room.

Apá sleeps on the sofa.

I tiptoe to the kitchen.

After volunteering
at the church,
Amá usually visits
my aunt Rosario,
and they play lotería.

I don't know how
she doesn't get bored
doing the same thing
every weekend.

Cleaning, babysitting,
volunteering, and familying.

I open the fridge.
Apá's hefty body
moves for a second,
then he keeps sleeping.

I want to ask him
for permission to leave
the apartment.
Then I realize
he wouldn't notice
anyway.

Nothing
seems to matter to him
these days.

As long as
I get home before Amá,
everything will be fine.

I grab my journal
and leave home.

ALISON'S HOUSE

I head to Alison's,
which is only a few blocks
from mine.

The mellow pink clouds
mix with the blue sky
as I walk past the park
that divides   our neighborhood.

I knock on
the mosquitera door.

Gustavo,
Alison's mother's boyfriend,
comes close.

He wears
a sleeveless T-shirt
and ripped old jeans.

She's not here,
he immediately says
when he sees my face.

Baby Leonardo
is crying behind him.

Leonardo has
the same big, brown
honey eyes as
Alison.

Amá calls him
el bebé chamagoso
'cause he's always
filthy and has runny eyes.

He hasn't quit
the pacifier,
and he's more than
three now.

I assume
Alison's mom
is not at home.

*Do you know if
she's working?*
I ask Gustavo.

He scratches his head
with this *who*
confused expression.

*Um, Alison.
Is she working?*
I ask again.

Guess so.
He shrugs.
Maybe she doubled shift.
I don't know.

Gustavo lights up
a cigarette.

Who is it?
A voice shouts
from below.

Alison's mom
is there inside.
Tavo turns his head.

Hey, man. You better go.
We're in the middle
of something.

I don't wanna know
what he's referring to.
If I were Alison,
I would hate him, too.

ARVIN'S ARID SUMMER

I don't want to go home yet.
I sit on a bench and open up
my journal instead.

The summer heat floats
over Las Palmas Park.
The air is hot and dry.

Skaters hang out.
People walk
their dogs around.

In the grass, babies swing
toward their moms.
They come and go,
come and go.

I think of
poor baby Leonardo.
Nobody will miss him
if Alison and I
take him with us one day.

All of a sudden,
someone
covers my eyes.

I KNOW THAT SMELL

Paris Hilton cheap perfume.

Alison, I know that's you.

Alison cracks up.
Her laugh is wildly fun.

She says,
What are you doing here alone?
Waiting for your Príncipe Azul?

The air blows her ironed hair.

I say,
Estás loca! Wait, you high?

She laughs hard and plops
her head on my legs.

Of course not.
I wish I were though.

I say,
I went to your house.

She frowns.
You did?

I nod.
Where were you?

She sits up straight.
I was at Ruben's.

I cover my face
with the notebook.

She laughs again.

Ruben is her "better than nothing."
He's 18 and lives
three houses away from me.

He doesn't attend school.
Ruben works whenever he wants.

I always tell Alison
she deserves better,
but she turns a deaf ear.

*I just don't like to be at home
when Tavo-jerk is there.*

Fair enough,
I say.

She continues,
And Tyler keeps ignoring me, so…

Talking about idiots.
I roll my eyes.

ALISON WAS THE FIRST ONE

who talked to me at school.

She didn't know
I was gay back then.

The first time
she said hello,
I felt she was trying
to hook up with me.

Then we talked
about famous Latinas
like Paulina Rubio and Shakira,
and she figured out who I was.

Amá told me not to trust
anyone except my family
with my secret.

But as Alison and I became friends,
she felt like a sister.
So eventually I shared more than
just laughs in the halls.

When someone put a note
on my locker that said,
I know you're queer
(99 percent sure it was Tyler,
the most popular guy in school),

Alison was there,
helping me to face
my fears and hold my
head up high.

I'm aware I promised Alex
not to tell anyone his secret.

But Alison is the ONLY ONE
who knows about
my feelings for him.

Besides, I'd rather talk
about Alex and me
than Amá's punishment.
Or that it baffles me how
Apá is quiet all the time.

PIZZA & FÚTBOL

Dusk falls in town.
The moon begins to lean out
on the horizon.

The air gets cold,
so I come home.

Amá isn't here yet.
Apá is still on the sofa.

This time he's watching
El Clásico del Fútbol Mexicano.
Basically, the two most popular soccer teams
in Mexico facing each other.

He has a dark beer on the table.

I know how much he would like
some pizza for dinner,
almost as much as I would.

I kindly ask
if we can order one.
He nods and hands me
a few dollars, but warns me
not to tell Amá.

First,
because
I'm grounded.

Second,
Amá hates when we eat
greasy stuff or,
as she calls it,
"trash food."

And even though
I don't like soccer,
I stay seated
next to Apá.

We may have stopped
doing puzzles together,
but at least
there is one thing
that still keeps us

TOGETHER
as a team.

SOCCER GAME FINISHES

at eight.

Apá is already lying flat
on his back.
He snores peacefully.

It makes me feel sad
seeing him like this.
Beer bottles and
wadded-up napkins
on the ground.

Although
it makes things easier
this way because
I don't need to ask him
for permission.

Amá is pretty
unpredictable
when she's with
my aunt Rosario.

She might come home
right now,
or she might not come
until 11.

On Saturday nights,
you never know.

I clean a little bit
and then go outside.

I get rid of
the empty pizza box
before she gets home.

ONLY THE BIKE

A brand-new bike is parked
outside Alex's apartment.

I remember what
Alex said the other night.
Are you down for a bike ride?

The worst part is
I don't have a decent one.

My old bike
needs tons of repair.
Also, it needs to be painted.

It was a gift
from my aunt Rosario's
husband.

He bought that
secondhand bike
for working out.

He never used it,
so he passed it to me.

Until one day,
the brakes suddenly failed
when I was on my way
to school.

I don't see Alex around.

I guess it's still early.
And I don't want to stand
over his dad's front door.
That would be too awkward.

It would be so much easier
if I had his number.

I sigh.

When I'm halfway
down the stairs,
I turn my face down,
but no trace
of Alex or his dad.

Only the bike.

UNGROUNDED

The sky is still gloomy
when I look out
the living room window
the next morning.

I put my face
against it.
And of course,
the bike is no longer there.

I feel guilty and dumb
for not being brave enough
to knock on
Alex's dad's door
last night.

Sometimes I wish I was
more like Alison.
She doesn't care
what other people think.

As soon as Amá wakes up,
the morning noise starts.

She turns the TV on
and then cleans out
the cabinets fast.

My phone lies
on the kitchen table,
which means
I'm no longer being punished.

That's how things work
with Amá.

She won't tell me
through words.
Just small actions that tell me
I have been ungrounded.

AMÁ ANNOUNCES

she will only work
a part shift today and that
when she gets home,
we'll head out to the mall.
Amá says I need
new shoes and a
decent pair of pants
for Daniela's quinceañera.

Daniela is
my aunt Rosario's daughter.
She's turning 15.

Like almost
every Mexican mother,
my aunt firmly believes
she must throw all her money
at her daughter's quince party.

Daniela is a good girl.
Smart and determined.
She wants to be a teacher
like her mom.

So I'm not sure
if she agreed to a huge party
because she's cool with the idea
or just to make
her mom happy.

MORNING SHOW

While Amá
puts her work shoes on,
she's watching a boring
TV morning show
with Apá.

One of the guests
is a man in his 40s
who talks about
how deeply in love
he is with his partner.

The projector screen
shows photos of
the two men with their kids.

Amá gets this disgusted face
and makes the sign of the cross.
Ay, Dios,
this shouldn't air during
children's viewing time!

APÁ DRIVES

to the Bakersfield outlet mall.

We barely have
10 minutes inside the car.

But I feel like
it was a MISTAKE
to have come after
Amá finished working.

Apá tells her
it's late and that
when we get there,
everything will be
CLOSED.

*If you had a job,
I wouldn't have
to work so much,*
Amá complains.

Apá tells her
that she doesn't appreciate
the fact he came home.

If I had known
they were going to fight
the entire time,
I would've taken the bus.

NOTHING FITS

I'm so skinny
that nothing fits me.
The pants look baggy
on me.

Amá says
I don't eat well.
And I want to say:

        You won't even let me
        eat pizza or hot dogs.

Apá says
I will look handsome
para las muchachas.
And I want to say:

        What girls
        are you talking about?
        I like boys.

But I keep quiet,
looking at myself in the mirror,
defeated.

WHEN I GET OUT OF THE CAR

another one
pulls up
next to ours,
in the apartment complex
parking lot.

Alex's eyes
brighten up.
He waves and
gets out.

My hands and
armpits sweat.

Amá looks
his way.
She has no choice
but to say hello.

Alex sticks out
a hand to Apá.

Alex Cisneros.
I'm Edgar's
classmate, sir,
he says confidently.

Pedro Jimenez,
Apá says with a
firm handshake.

I help Amá
get some bags
from the trunk.

She got paid today,
so we bought
grocery stuff.

Apá's all smiles
while talking to Alex
about soccer.

When Amá and I finish,
Apá closes the car.

Nice to see you again,
Mrs. Jimenez,
Alex says.
Amá half-smiles.

She HATES
when people call her
Mrs. Jimenez.
She says
she's not
Apá's property.

I want to
crack up.

ALEX OFFERS TO HELP

take the bags upstairs.
To *my* apartment.

My face turns red.
I don't want him to see
the place where I live.

I mean,
his dad is living
in this building too,
but Alex isn't.

I don't want to be
the broke guy for him.
But it's too late, 'cause
Amá says,
It would do us well to have
another pair of hands.
Since Pedro hurt his leg working,
it hasn't been the same.

Suddenly, I get it.

Apá lost his job
'cause they felt he wasn't
strong enough
to do the work.
My heart clenches,
and I want to
give Apá a hug.

But then he says
out of the blue,
*Are you guys
gonna hang out?*

Alex and I nod.

Amá gives me a look.
Edgar, don't be late.

ALEX TELLS HIS DAD

that he's with a boy
from school.

It seems so simple
for him.

While I wait outside,
I text Alison.

> *I ran into Alex.*
> *We are going for a walk.*
> *Am I on a date? lol*

My heart flutters
as I text.

She quickly responds
with a few kissy
and devil emojis.

YESSSS. You're off
on a date! My baby
has grown.

THE D-ROUTE

The night is perfect.
It's not too warm,
not too cold.

We decide to go
walking instead of
driving around.

Is your dad OK?
I ask.

What do you mean?
he asks.

*You know, 'cause
you came to visit him,
and now you're hanging out
with me,* I say.

He shrugs.
*He and my mom
are having a rough time.
I guess he only wants
my siblings and me
to be happy.*

I'm sorry,
I say.

Alex says,
It's OK.
They had
an awful relationship
anyway.

I think of
my parents' relationship,
 which is   f   a   r
 from perfect.

This whole divorce thing
has been harsh,
Alex adds.
They still have a lot
of paperwork to do.

I think of
my parents' immigration status.

I nod, a little embarrassed.

Very deep inside,
I hope my parents don't take the D-route.

FUEGO PARENTS

We get to the park.
It's empty and dark.

The stars hang
like lamps in the sky.

We sit
on the grass.
Crickets chirping
is the only sound.

Alex finally speaks.
Just so you know,
I brought my bike
the other day.

My chest tightens.

I'm so sorry. I just…
I didn't…
I was grounded and…

Alex laughs.
Hey, it's OK.
He puts a hand
on my shoulder.

I assumed you were
busy or something,
but grounded?

The truth sounds
too pathetic to explain.
I only say,
My parents think I'm rude.

He says,
Don't all parents think
that about their children?

I answer,
I guess, but mine explode
even for the tiniest things.

He grins.
Tyler thinks
Mexican parents
are a little bit
dramatic.

He doesn't get
how Mexicans are
'cause hc's white,
I think to myself.

I try to wipe away
those words
from my head.

I let out a deep sigh.
Well, my bike
doesn't work anyway.
Forgot to tell you that day.

Alex shakes his head,
letting out a laugh.

FIRST DATE

When I was a kid,
I thought my first date
would be a cute girl.
I'd be wearing a nice shirt.

I was wrong.

It's actually
at the nearest McDonald's
with a hot dude.
And I'm wearing my old jeans.

Burgers and fries
with another guy—
all the things Amá
would disapprove of.

This one's on me,
Alex says when we
order our combos.

I want to say no
but murmur, *Thanks.*

We mostly talk
about school and our goals.
He hopes to get
a football scholarship.
I share what my parents think
about my writer's dream.

Suddenly, his phone buzzes
on the table.

I gotta take this call,
he says, suddenly sounding
worried.

Hey, Max!
he says.

He listens and nods.
Just go to bed, buddy,
he says softly.
I'll be there,
like, in an hour, OK?

Alex hangs up.
It was my little brother.
He sighs.
After my parents split,
he's had a hard time
falling asleep.

My sister is a strong girl,
but Max...
He shakes his head.
Guess he misses having
Dad around.

I don't want to be nosy,
but I ask,
What about your mom?

He says,
She's dealing with
her own...stuff.

Hope everything's fine,
I say.

He gives a little smile.

I slide open my phone
and text Alison,
        This is officially
        my first date.

LEGENDS

Lights go red.
We cross the street.

So, how are those poems going?
Alex asks me.

They're good,
I say. Surprised that he asked.

He nudges me.
Can I get a small preview?

Maybe later,
I say. I go red, too.

He studies my face.
Hmm, OK.

I cave.
*Have you heard
the legend of the lovers,
the Moon and the Sun?*

Alex hesitates.
I guess?

I tease him.
Which one of all the versions?

He pauses and thinks.
Then blurts out,
OK, I lied! I don't know the story.

I laugh.
*How is it possible
that you don't know that legend?*

He shrugs.
*It's not something like
they teach us at school.*

Well, Mexican grandmoms always tell it,
I say.

He scratches his hair.
My grandma is dead.

My stomach drops.
I am sorry, I—

It's OK, he says.
She died before I was born.

Alex falls silent,
and I feel I ruined our first date.
So, what are you waiting for?
he asks.

Waiting...?
I ask, confused.

To tell me a legend.

I smile.
Come with me.

RABBIT IN THE MOON

We step into
the playground area.

I climb on the slide.
Alex does the same.

I decide which story
I want to tell him.

We lie on our backs.
Everything is still,
so I begin.

Quetzalcóatl,
god of the Cosmos,
once went to travel
the world.

As the evening fell,
he felt tired and hungry
but kept walking.
Then he met a bunny
that had come out to eat grass.

Alex listens carefully.

The bunny invited him
to share his food,
but the god said
he didn't eat grass,
and he would most likely die
of hunger that night.

The bunny said,
"Eat me. I am nothing more
than a rabbit."

Quetzalcóatl gently stroked
the rabbit and said,
"You may not be more than a bunny,
but everyone will remember you."

He raised him to the moon,
where his figure was stamped,
and said,
"I will put your portrait here
for all humanity to see. Forever."

We stay silent
for a moment.

Then Alex asks, surprised,
Wait, did you make up
that story?

I laugh softly.
I told you—it's a legend.

His mouth falls open.
Well, it's awesome.
I should share that story
with Max whenever
he can't sleep.

LOVERS AND BUNNIES

Monday and Tuesday fly by.
On Wednesday,
I have two text messages.

One from Alison
and one from Alex.

I open his first.
Can't wait for version two
of that legend!
Is it with lovers
or more bunnies?

I smirk.

Alison says she wants
to talk.

    Only if you bring
    a free meal,
    I respond.

Deal!

THE PARTY

My parents aren't home.
They went to visit
my uncles to tell them
the news.

Apá finally
got the job in
the grape field.

Alison puts the burger
and fries on the table.
I kiss the bag.

She rolls her eyes.
Seriously, I don't understand
your fascination
with this food.
It makes me sick.

I laugh.
So, what's up?
What you wanna talk
about?

Tyler is throwing a party,
she starts.

You know, the one he always
gives before back to school.
Didn't Alex say
anything to you?

I try to hide
my disappointment,
and grab some fries.

I haven't spoken to Alex
since our date,
I lie.

I can tell she doesn't believe me.
Well, the party is
this Friday. You down?

I shake my head no.
You know
I don't like Tyler
after that note
he put on my locker.
He doesn't
even like me!

Alison rolls her eyes.
Let it go, Edgar.
It was a long time ago.
Plus, you're not even
sure it was him!

It was him! I insist.
*I recognized that awful
handwriting.*

Alison ignores me
'cause she knows
I'm right.
Please?
Everyone will be there.
Alex will be there, too,
she winks.

Ugh, OK, I'll think about it,
I say.

LIAR

Alison has convinced me
to go to the party.
But convincing Amá
is not that easy.

*Amá, Alison is already
waiting outside,* I say.

She holds firm.
*I don't care. The president
could be waiting for you,
and you still wouldn't go.*

Please, I beg.

*No, Edgar. Who knows
what people do
at those parties?*

After eight missed calls
from Ali and almost
getting down on my knees,

Apá asks,
*Is that Alison
your girlfriend?*

Umm…yeah, I lie.
My palms sweat.

*See, Lidia? Let him go.
Edgar has to meet girls.*

Amá keeps quiet.
She knows I'm a liar.

THE ONLY REASON

Alison came tonight
is because she wants
to see Tyler.

Palm trees surround
the two-story house.

We walk inside.

Alison looks for Tyler.
She can't find him,
so we decide to hang out
in the living room.

We meet
my cousin Daniela.
She never comes
to parties, but all
the schoolkids are here
tonight.

She talks
about her quinceañera
over and over again.
She sounds excited.

For a moment,
I forget that I am
at Tyler's.

For a moment,
I even forget
what Tyler did.

(I know you're queer.
The words haunted me
for months.)

Want a drink?
Alison asks.

I don't want to be
a killjoy, so I nod.

She walks to the kitchen
with Daniela, and
they leave me alone.

FEEL THE MOMENT

The music is loud.
Guys are already wasted.
They take selfies
and joke around.

I take out my phone
to check if Amá has called,
but there are no calls.
I turn my phone OFF.

I want to chill out
and have some fun.
I don't wanna think
about my parents or
my dirty white shoes.

Suddenly, I see him:
ebony hair
and brown-hazel eyes.

Alex glances around.

It's as if he's looking
for something.
Maybe for someone?
Until his gaze pauses
on me.

My heart races
when I see his dimples.
I give him a smile.

He waves over
and walks through
the crowd.

Hola,
he says.

Hi,
I say.

I want
to ask Alex why
he didn't mention
the party.

But a wide smile
crosses his face.
And I can't think
of anything else.

ALISON SHOWS UP

with two red cups
and gives me one.

She squeezes my shoulder
and smiles at Alex.
He starts talking about football.

I sip my drink.
It tastes too sour.
I wanna spit it out.

I hope Alison
doesn't get too wasted.
Sometimes she
can't control her mouth.

After too much football talk,
she leaves us alone.

I FINISH MY DRINK

Alex asks me
if I want another one.

I really don't,
but I nod.
I want to impress him.

We make our way
to the kitchen.

I see some familiar faces
but try to ignore them.

We grab our drinks
from a table full of bottles
of who-knows-what.

This one tastes strong.
Tequila, I think, as the drink
burns in my throat.

A band starts playing.
People cheer
from the yard.

Alex and I join
the pulsing crowd.

NEON LIGHTS

flood the wooden stage
and the pool.

The girl from the band sings,
Promise me the coast is clear.

Alex's eyes spark
when they meet mine,
brighter than
a dozen lights.

Let me keep you warm.
People sing the lyrics
along with the band.

When the second song begins,
Alex wants to go
for another drink.

As we walk,
I feel a pair of eyes
staring at us.

Hey! Wait,
someone shouts.

We turn our heads.

Tyler is standing there.
He wraps his arm
around Alison's shoulder.

TRUTH

Alex looks ashamed.
Like he's trying to
hide himself.

It's too late to run away.
Tyler calls
our names.

I didn't know you two
were friends.
He stretches out
the word "friends."

I can smell
his alcohol breath
from here.

No, we aren't,
Alex says, quickly.

No more wide smiles
or sparks in his eyes.

He just lives
in the same building
as, um—

*Why didn't you tell me
you were hanging out
with this dude?*
Tyler interrupts.

Alison, also drunk,
asks Tyler to stop.
C'mon, let's go inside.

But Tyler won't stop.
*Hey, Edgar,
truth or dare?*

Truth, truth, truth!
shout Jorge and Steve,
two guys
from the football team.
They raise their glasses
like this is a fun game.

Tyler, please,
Alison repeats.

*Man, I don't have
anything against homos,
you know,
but is it true
you like dudes?*
He asks, as if there's
something wrong with that.

My mouth goes dry and
I drop my eyes to the
G
R
O
U
N
D.

Alex doesn't say
or do anything.
Why would he?

So obviously he wasn't the one
to tell Tyler.

Suddenly,
everything clicks.

Alison was THE ONE
who knew.

Alison was THE ONE
who told Tyler
the truth.

NIGHTMARE

I feel like I'm in a nightmare
where I can't run away.

More people
gather around.

So is it true you're into Alex?
Tyler blurts out
and smacks my butt.

Leave him alone, Ty,
someone from the crowd shouts.

That's n-not your business,
I stutter.

People clap
and laugh.

I don't know what to do,
so my body reacts for me.
I quicken my pace
to the patio door
without looking back.

I TRY TO IGNORE

Alex, Tyler,
and everyone.

I try to ignore
the awkward moment
from tonight.

I try to ignore
Alison's voice
shouting my name.

She will be OK.
I know Daniela
will take care of her.

But I can't ignore
the embarrassment.
The pain inside.

TEARS

blur my vision
as I walk the lonely,
dark streets.

The night gets cold.
At least I brought
my red jacket.

I shouldn't have come.
I shouldn't have come.
Amá was right.

When I'm far enough,
I lean against a tree.
It feels like too much
to handle.

And finally,
after all these months,
I cover my face
and let myself cry.

I WAKE UP AT SIX

No messages on my phone.
I go back to sleep.

I wake up at eight.

I hear Amá complain about
how much Apá
drank last night.

I go back to sleep.

HANGOVER

Amá is washing the dishes
Finally, you woke up!
It's past eleven,
she says, her arms up.
Are you hungover?

I don't feel like arguing,
so I keep my mouth shut.

You hungry?

I shake my head.

Maybe some green enchiladas?
Your favorites? she insists.

I sigh quietly.
No, Amá, no!

¡Uy, qué carácter!
See? That's how hangovers feel.

How do I explain to her
it's not my bad temper
but an emotional hangover?

SUNDAY IS

tons of Alison's
missed calls
and unopened messages.

Sunday is
staying in bed.

Sunday is
feeling hurt.

Tomorrow
will be worse.

I will go back to school
and face the truth.
Even when all I want
is to stay here,
alone in my room.

I don't know what else
to do.
So I write a poem
for Alex:

"ONLY PIECES"

a poem by Edgar Jimenez

We passed through
the shadows and the sounds
from the park that night.
It reminded me
how happiness felt.

I thought
we were pieces
coming together.
Never imagined
we were falling apart.

But I guess we are
only pieces
looking for a place
in the universe.

And maybe
you haven't found
that place yet.
I hope you do.

I hope you find
that place
where you belong.

FIRST DAY

Yellow morning light
hits me in the face.
I get ready for school
after summer break.

Apá gets ready
for his first workday
in el campo.

A pan dulce basket,
coffee, and orange juice
sit on the table.

Amá brings up
Alex's dad.
*The vecinos think
he's raro.*

I say, *Just because
he doesn't talk with you all
doesn't mean he's weird.*

Amá sips her coffee.
*Apparently, he only goes
to work and then
hides in that apartment
all day.*

So, you guys spy on him?!
I ask.

Apá sighs, tired already.

Amá ignores my question
and asks, *You OK?*

I shrug.
Just a little bit stressed.

In my time,
nobody had time to be
stressed,
Amá says.

I WALK

through the
crowded halls.

I'm glad
Alison, Alex, and Tyler
are not around.

I'm
a nervous wreck
and don't want
to throw up
the pan dulce
in front of them.

MY FIRST CLASS

is literature.

Mr. Evans asks us
to write an essay
about what seasons
mean for us.

Thirty minutes later,
he asks who wants
to read their first lines
out loud.

He stares at me.
He knows
I love writing,
but today
I try to keep
a low profile.

I keep writing a poem
in my journal
all through English,
and then in math
as Ms. Gutiérrez
tries to explain geometry.

"RIVER OVER ME"

a poem by Edgar Jimenez

I hate when
I feel this way.
When I want to
enjoy something:
a class, a book,
a geometry problem,
and simply can't.

The feeling runs
through my body.
It boards, it kayaks,
it overflows.

Sometimes it moves
too fast,
and my unwieldy body
can't swim anymore.

Other days
it dries up.
Sometimes anger and sadness
are the only waters
I can dive in.

I guess they are
all I've ever known.

I'M TOO DEEP

in my thoughts.
I don't realize
Ms. Gutiérrez
is next to me.

The whole class
bursts out laughing.

I hand her my notebook,
and she reads
CAREFULLY.

Then she writes
something on it.
If it's a note for Amá,
I'm screwed.

When the class is over,
I take a look at her lines:

You have talent, kiddo.
I suggest you read
Franny Choi
and Juan Felipe Herrera.

IGNORED

During lunch,
I don't know where to go.

I take out a coke
from the vending machine.

All of a sudden,
I see his burnt-caramel skin.
Alex passes down the hall
looking the other way
on purpose.

I stand there awkwardly,
but he pretends
not to see me.

THE CAFETERIA FILLS

with whispers
as I walk in.
Maybe it's just
my imagination.

I sit in the corner
where two friends
are talking about
Netflix shows while
they unpack their lunch.

Completely unexpected,
someone comes up
behind me
and gently taps on
my shoulder.

Hi,
says Alison.

I TRIED TO CALL YOU

she says softly.

I didn't want to talk,
I respond.

She tries to reach out.
I am sorry for everything.
For telling Tyler something
I shouldn't have.
For not being there
when you needed me . . .

I turn away.
Do you realize all the stress
you put me through?
We were supposed to be
FRIENDS.

She holds back her tears.
I know, I know.
Look, I just wanted
to give you something.

I shake my head.
I need to go to class.
She reaches for my hand
and places a half-moon
silver pendant in it.

I have the other half.
She knows how much
I love the sun, the moon,
and the stars.

I half-smile.

You know I'm not
the type of person who apologizes.
But I'm deeply sorry, Edgar.
I really am.
This last day has been awful
without you.

I hug Alison.

Tears run down her cheeks.

Hey, it's OK.
You were super drunk,
so it doesn't count, OK?

She laughs and cries
at the same time.
You're a better friend
than I am.

People are looking at us.
But I couldn't care less
this time.

I HAVEN'T TALKED

with Tyler since that night,
Alison says as we walk
away from school.

I nudge her.
You OK?

She shrugs.
I'm alright. I'm glad
I didn't…
She shakes her head.
I feel like a fool.
I stayed at Daniela's.
Your cousin's cool.

I'm glad she was there.

Alison nods.
Now, ready for some greasy food?

I laugh.
Always ready.

THE QUINCEAÑERA DAY ARRIVES

I didn't want to come,
but Amá forced me to.

I love my cousin.
It's just I prefer
to keep my distance
from my relatives.

Plus, I hate wearing
formal clothes.

We walk into the party hall.
It's decorated
with purple helium balloons
and fake pink roses.

A Tigres del Norte
song comes ON.

We sit at
one of the tables with
bright pink tablecloths.

My uncle Jorge,
Daniela's dad,
reaches over.
He's wearing
a sombrero hat.

He chats
with Apá first.
Then he asks me,
Pá cuándo la novia, mijo?

He always finds ways
to make me feel
uncomfortable.

Asking when I will
have a girlfriend
is one of them.

Thank God
Daniela shows up.
People clap
and whistle.

She looks stunning.

No glasses or the
white sneakers
she usually wears.

Instead, a cute purple dress
that highlights
her curves.
A silver tiara
on her head.

ALISON TEXTS ME

She asks
if Alex has reached out.

Amá says
I should stop texting.

Daniela dances
with her chambelanes,
her quince court.

Aunt Rosario cries.

Alison keeps texting me.
You should call Alex.

The party emcee DEMANDS
relatives dance
with the quinceañera.

Amá glances at me.

No way,
I say.
I hate dancing.

Don't be rude.
It's your cousin. So go.

More notifications
from Alison.

I know Amá won't let it go,
so I breathe deeply
and walk toward Daniela.

I COUNT MY STEPS

as we dance.

One, two, three, turn.

So, how's Alison?
Daniela asks.

She's fine, I say. *Thank you,
prima, for that night.
Guess she learned
drinking that much
is never a good idea.*

*I hope you learned
your lesson, too,*
Daniela says.

One, two, three, turn.

I frown.
What you mean?

*There will be more
Tylers in your life,*
she says.

*But you always need
to remind yourself
how special you are.
Never be ashamed of that.*

We stop for a moment.

I wrap Daniela
in a big, big hug.
Gracias.

People clap even though
they don't know
what's going on.

You know you have my support,
she says warmly.
*And talk to your dad
only when you're ready.*

I nod.
*You look beautiful,
by the way.*

She giggles.
Thanks, primo.
As I get close to my table,
Apá is staring at me
with this severe look
I've never seen before.

He holds my phone.

DANG.

I forgot to lock my phone.

He read my texts
with Alison.

MY FIRST REACTION

is to walk away—very fast.
Just like that night
at the party.

Amá calls out my name,
but the people gather
and the event staff
divide   us.

I accidentally hit
a woman
holding a soda.
It spills all over.

I'm sorry!
I yell.

One, two,
three,
four blocks.

I take a couple
deep breaths.

I turn.

I don't see
Amá or Apá
anymore.

I don't know
where to go.

I could hide
in the park.

But that wouldn't
work forever.

Tired and defeated,
I just go home.

BREATHE IN, BREATHE OUT

I breathe in.

What am I gonna say
when my parents arrive?

Is Apá going to
kick me out of the house?
Will he beat me up?
My stomach growls.

Someone knocks
on the door,
pulling me out of
my thoughts.

I feel spaced out.

I take a loooong
deep breath before
opening the door.

Alex Cisneros
is standing there.
Cool if I come in?

I know
this isn't a good time,
but my heart keeps
popping up like popcorn
in a heavy-bottomed pot.

I can't ignore
how he makes me feel,
so I just step outside.

I breathe out.

SOMEBODY

Alex drives
until we stop
in an empty
parking lot.

We sit
on the hood
of his Altima.

Look,
I'm sorry for
telling Alison about
your parents' situation,
I start.

He shrugs.
Isn't that
what friends do?
Gossip?

I say,
I guess?

We both smile.

I'm the one
who should apologize.
For not defending you
at the party.
For looking away at school,
pretending nothing happened.
I was so scared.

His eyes glow under
the moon.
And in this moment,
all I can see
is his honesty.

I know
what Tyler did
was terribly wrong.
But he was like
a brother to me,
you know?

I nod.

He continues,
Family has always been
everything to me.
And when mine broke apart—
Tyler was there.
But things haven't been
the same since that night.
He snorts,
shaking his head.

*We exchange
some words
after practice,
but that's all.*

Alex pauses
and then asks,
So, is it true?

I act like I don't know what
he's talking about.
What do you mean?

You know, he says.
About your crush.

I look the other way.
Yes. It is true.

He nods slowly.

I can feel
my face flushing.
*Can I ask you
something?*

He stares at me.
Sure.

Would you…
…date a guy?

Alex sighs.
Not sure.
It's not that
easy, OK?

Then I understand.
I thought Alex
was my first date.
But maybe Alex isn't
somebody
I could have
a date with.

I remember
the poem I wrote.
Alex is like a missing piece.
But hearts are more complicated
than puzzles.

Maybe he just
hasn't found
his way out yet.

But I don't want
to be somebody
hidden or
somebody I am not.
I want to be me.
I'm ready
to get out
from the shadows.

Then it hits me.

I also wrote
that poem for myself.

I was a
missing piece, too.

I know what
I need to do.

*Alex, I have
to head home.*

THE APARTMENT
LIGHTS ARE ON

My parents have arrived.

Alex turns off his car.

By the way,
I called you,
he says.

WHEN?
I ask.

Before coming tonight,
he answers.

WHAT?

Yeah. Your dad picked up.
Why did he have your phone?
Alex laughs.

I'm all serious.
What did he say?

Nothing much, Alex says.
*He was a little short
with me.
Sounded very different
from the day I met him.*

I get out of the car.
Talk to you later.

Alex says something,
but I can't hear.

I'm already
running up the stairs.

A DIFFERENT LIFE

Amá is folding clothes
in the living room.

She doesn't even ask
where I was.

Apá is watching TV.

It's so hard to breathe.

Can we talk?
I ask him.

Apá lets out a snort.

*I know you already know, but
I wanted to say that I…am…
I hope you…*

Apá turns the TV off.

*I don't
fully comprehend, Edgar.*
His eyes still
on the screen.

You never liked girly stuff,
like Barbie dolls or
playing with a kitchen set.
All this time,
I pictured a different life for you.

Maybe you never
really knew me,
I think to myself.

Could you at least
look me in the eye?
My voice trembles.

Could you tell me
at least why you're "this"?
he asks.

Why is it so hard for him
to say the word?

Your mom and I
gave you everything.

I say,
That's the problem, Apá.

Giving you everything?
he says.

I shake my head.
No, Apá. The problem is
you think being gay
is a problem.

Edgar, please.
Amá gets closer, like
she's scared that my quiet dad,
who finally spoke, could slap me.

Well, I have nothing
else to say,
Apá says firmly
and turns on the TV again.

Apá?
I am GAY,
and "this" won't go away.
I wanna know.
Are you going
to love me the same?

Edgar…
Amá sobs
and puts her hand
on my shoulder.

I shake her
hand away.

Apá turns his head.
I would never hate you.
You're my son.

But that's not the answer
I wanted to hear.

I hope you could
give it a try.
'Cause I do love you, Apá,
I say,
holding back tears.

He closes his eyes
and breathes out.

A LIGHT

Amá puts
my folded clothes
on the bed.

I pretend I'm OK.

But when
she leans against me,
all that comes out
are tears.

Shh. It's OK, mijo.
There's no reason to cry.
It's OK.
Her voice softens.

I rest my head
on her shoulder
and can't stop crying.

Ay, Edgar,
give your dad some time.
Try to understand.
It's not easy for him
either. For us.

I anchor myself
in my mom's arms.

We love you.
We will always love you.
We had a rough time
before you were born,
she sniffs.

And then
you brought light
into our lives.
That's why we only want
you to be happy.

And I hope I will be, too.

CONSTELLATION

Alex calls me,
but I don't respond.

I quickly text,
telling him I can't
talk right now.

Amá doesn't leave
me alone until I pretend
I'm falling asleep.

At least
she seems better
with me being gay.

I read Alex's response.
How did everything go?

> *Still @ home.*
> *My dad didn't kick me out*
> *or worse.*
> *I've heard many stories*
> *at school from other*
> *gay kids.*

Give him time.

Do I have a choice?

Lol! Meet up tomorrow?

Only if we go for tacos.

I hate tacos!

What Mexican hates tacos?!

Me? :P

Weird

*Just cuz I don't like
meat inside a tortilla?*

I imagine Alex laughing
as he texts, and I laugh too.

Text you tomorrow then.

Good night, Moon.

I laugh again.
The glisten of the moon
brings me close to
the window.

But it's the stars' position
in the sky,
their constant motion,
that makes me think
about what Alex feels.
And how all his insecurities
could move away
tomorrow.

I guess
I should at least
give us a chance.

Night, Rabbit.

"FIREFLIES"

a poem by Edgar Jimenez

Reading through
the pages of my journal
and watching this
town as it sleeps
makes me think

how different
life would be
if I hadn't let go of
the fear of
coming out as I am.

If I had lived
the life Apá designed
for me while
we were building puzzles
when I was a child.

If I hadn't talked
with Alex about
our hopes and dreams

while showing him how
moon and stars shine
equally bright
in the sky.

If I hadn't understood
that Amá is only afraid of
seeing me suffer
when I thought
she was being harsh.

But now I know
they were showing me
they CARE
in many different ways.

And I want to give them
all my love
from a place
where I can be me.
Always being me.

From this place
where I can feel
a thousand luciérnagas
flying inside my heart,
free from the hurt.

WANT TO KEEP READING?

If you liked this book, check out another
book from West 44 Books:

RISING OUT
BY *M. AZMITIA*

ISBN: 9781978595439

PART ONE

The Plan

♀

The first time I
saw Eri,

tumbling
onto the grass at
the park near our
homes,

she was a boy
named Maurice.

She screamed as
she fell.

    The Band-Aid
across her nose was
too light.

    Tan on deep, dark
brown skin.

I watched her
blood seep through
the Band-Aid.

Watched it
smear with dirt as
she fell again. But

she screamed

and laughed

and stood up again.

I loved her
before I ever knew
what that meant.

◗

I should not
have been born.

I should have been
a dream forgotten,
set aside.

A split from
this timeline.

A *what if?*

A footnote
in my family
tree.

I was the thing that made
my mother morning-sick.

I was the thing that
nearly killed her
upon arrival.

Or maybe I was
the thing she
sacrificed to stay
alive.

But was it worth it?

I lived, but
there would be
a price.

♀

I grew up knowing
I would need to be

better.

That's the order
of things.

       Isn't it?

Mom does better
than Grandma.

I do better
than her.

We struggle
so the next of us
can step over us,

can go higher.

And *oh*,
did Mom struggle.

My mother's hands
have never been soft.

I've always known them
as strong.

Hard from the
work that kept her
away from me
for so much of her time.

Juggling time
at all her jobs.
At school.
At my side.

Hard from clawing
through the walls set
in her path.

Hard from burying
her dreams

so that I could chase
my own.

Rough when she
held my face
and looked me
in the eye.

Anaya, she'd say.
You need to do
better than me.

📍

She laid out
The Plan
for me

as soon as I could
understand what
she was saying.

- Stay in school.

- Get good grades.

- Don't get in trouble.

- Go to college.

- Get a job.

- Buy a car.

- Buy a house.

    - Then, if,

        and only *if*,

you meet a man

who can
give you something

that you just can't
get on your own:

- Marry him.
- Have a family.

Be happy in knowing
that you *won.*

*Don't make the same
mistakes I did,*
she'd say.

I knew what
she meant.

What she never said.

*Don't settle for someone
who can't give you
the life you deserve.*

*Don't leave your home
for a future so uncertain.*

*Don't start a family
you're not ready for.*

*Don't make a mistake that
will put your dreams on hold.*

Then she'd pull on
a work shirt.

One with a
store logo.

Or one that would
smell of cleaning
products when she
dragged herself home
in the morning.

Or one that would
be grease-stained
and stink of alcohol
when she got home
from tending bar.

And she'd leave me,

long after the sky
had darkened.

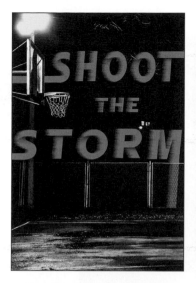

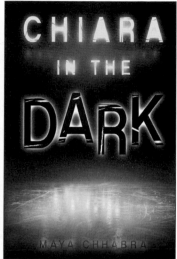

CHECK OUT MORE BOOKS AT:
www.west44books.com

An imprint of Enslow Publishing

WEST **44** BOOKS™

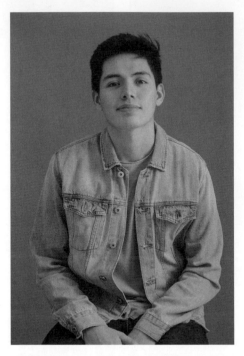

ABOUT THE AUTHOR

Edd Tello is a bilingual writer of children's and Young Adult literature. He has worked as an English teacher in Kindergarten and elementary schools.

Edd graduated from the University of Seville with a Master's in Creative Writing. Since then, he has been writing newsletters and articles for website publications.

He is currently a high school teacher in Mexico. *Only Pieces* is his debut YA novel.

When he isn't reading or writing, you can find him drinking coffee in the woods.

Please visit him online at eddtello.com and @eddstello.